FIREHOUSE 1
FIRE AT THE BAKERY

Written by Sadhna Sheli

Illustrated by Manuela Gutierrez

WEE SOLES BOOKS ★ LOS ANGELES

For Noah, Mary, Kai, and Tom
—Love, Mom

And to America's firefighters,
especially my cousin,
Fire Chief Bill Seng.
—XO Sadhna

Text and illustrations copyright © 2017 Sadhna Sheli
Illustrations by Manuela Gutierrez
Wee Soles Books logo - Illustration by Ed Rook
Design by Billie Jo Moscherosch
Firehouse 1 logo design by Billie Jo Moscherosch
Cover design by Billie Jo Moscherosch
Book design by Sonia Sparhawk
Editing by Lisa Rojany, Editorial Services of Los Angeles
Production by Caroline and Doug Bossi

Library of Congress Catalog Number: 2017907959
ISBN 978-0692877616
www.firehouse1kids.com

Printed in the United States of America.
1 3 5 7 9 10 8 6 4 2

It's a sunny morning at Firehouse 1.
The firefighters are busy checking and cleaning their trucks.

"Cleaning tires or fighting fires . . . oh yeah . . . we got it.
We're Firehouse 1," sings Max with a smile as he scrubs a dirty tire.
"Oh Max, you can turn any moment into a song," giggles Alex.

Suddenly they are interrupted by the fire bell.

"Emergency, emergency!
Fire at the bakery!"

Dispatcher Dan's voice booms over the loudspeaker.

"Alex and Eddie, bring the paramedic truck!"
"Molly, Bo, Max, and Cinder
take the engine.
I'll meet you there!"
orders Chief Goodman.

The firefighters rush to put on their protective gear and
climb aboard their vehicles.

They race down the street with their sirens blaring.
"Firehouse 1 is on the run!" they shout in unison.

Within moments they arrive at the bakery, where the police are already at the scene directing traffic and assisting people who have evacuated the bakery.

"Is everyone out of the building?" Chief Goodman asks Coco, the bakery owner.

"Yes, everyone is out and safe,"
Coco responds.

"Looks like you burned your hand, Coco.
Let's have firefighter Eddie take care of that for you,"
says Chief Goodman.

"Listen up, team!" says Chief Goodman.
"Max and Molly, hook up the engine to the hydrant.
I want everyone to go into the bakery
with their air packs on."

Molly finishes hooking up the hose and
uses her portable radio to call Max.
"I'm hooked up here, Max.
Turn on the hydrant when you're ready."

Bo and Alex are at the nozzle, and Molly helps them get the heavy hose into the building.

They slowly make their way through
the smoke-filled room
toward the back of the building.

Within moments they are lost.

"I can't see a thing through this smoke!"
says Bo.

"I'll radio for help," says Alex.

Says Alex into her radio.

"Hang tight. I'll send in Cinder to help,"
responds Chief Goodman.

"Cinder, I need you to go in and help the team locate the fire," orders Chief Goodman.

"Woof!"

Cinder barks in response and runs into the building.

"Woof!"

"Woof!"

"Woof!"

She immediately crouches down to crawl her way under the thick black smoke, barking to alert the firefighters.

Molly hears Cinder barking and shouts,
"We're over here, Cinder!"

Cinder carefully makes her way over to the firefighters and gently guides them to the kitchen where the fire is blazing.

The team begins to battle the fire by spraying water from the hose, when all of a sudden . . .

the burst of water from the hose turns into a trickle.
"What just happened?" asks Bo.

"Let's find out!" responds Molly.
"Cinder, we need you to check the hose!
We've lost pressure somehow."

Cinder crawls along the hose line and quickly discovers a kink in the hose. Using her strong teeth, she untangles the hose and heads back to check on the firefighters.

Alex is busy hammering away with her pike pole at the wall next to the oven to make sure the fire hasn't spread into the walls. Cinder helps by using her paws to remove the loose pieces.

Within minutes, the fire is out.
"We are good here!"
shouts Alex to Molly and Bo.

Alex radios Max. "Shut off the water!"

"Coco got lucky here.
Seems like the fire
was only in this
oven area," says Bo.

The firefighters pull the heavy hose out of the bakery.

"Fire's out, Chief," reports Bo.
"Cinder saved the day!" announces Molly.
"Great job, team!" says Chief Goodman.

"When someone's in trouble,
we're there on the double!"
the firefighters cheer.

"Thank you, Firehouse 1," says Coco.

"That's what we're here for, we're happy to help!"

says Chief Goodman.

Later back at Firehouse 1 it's time for dinner. "Cinder, you were a real hero today. And to show you my appreciation, I've got a bowl of juicy blueberries just for you," says Eddie.

"Woof!" "Woof!" "Woof!"

Cinder

Cinder barks happily in response.

"That sounds delicious, Eddie, but what's for us?
I'm starving!" says Max, rubbing his belly.
"Is there ever a time when you're not hungry?"
asks Eddie jokingly.

But before anyone gets a chance to eat . . .

The fire bell rings, and Dispatcher
Dan's voice booms over the loudspeaker.

Made in the USA
San Bernardino, CA
29 June 2017